Unicorn Princesses
FEATHER'S FLIGHT

The Unicorn Princesses series

Sunbeam's Shine

Flash's Dash

Bloom's Ball

Prism's Paint

Breeze's Blast

Moon's Dance

Firefly's Glow

Feather's Flight

Unicorn Princesses
FEATHER'S FLIGHT

Emily Bliss

illustrated by Sydney Hanson

BLOOMSBURY
CHILDREN'S BOOKS
NEW YORK LONDON OXFORD NEW DELHI SYDNEY

BLOOMSBURY CHILDREN'S BOOKS
Bloomsbury Publishing Inc., part of Bloomsbury Publishing Plc
1385 Broadway, New York, NY 10018

BLOOMSBURY, BLOOMSBURY CHILDREN'S BOOKS, and the Diana logo
are trademarks of Bloomsbury Publishing Plc

First published in the United States of America in August 2018
by Bloomsbury Children's Books
www.bloomsbury.com

Bloomsbury books may be purchased for business or promotional use. For information on
bulk purchases please contact Macmillan Corporate and Premium Sales Department at
specialmarkets@macmillan.com

Library of Congress Cataloging-in-Publication Data
Names: Bliss, Emily, author. | Hanson, Sydney, illustrator.
Title: Feather's flight / by Emily Bliss ; illustrated by Sydney Hanson.
Description: New York : Bloomsbury, 2018. | Series: Unicorn princesses ; 8
Summary: Cressida visits the Rainbow Realm where Feather, a unicorn who can fly,
is having a sleepover, complete with magic pajamas created by Ernest the wizard lizard
that will allow the others to fly.
Identifiers: LCCN 2018005074 (print) | LCCN 2018013252 (e-book)
ISBN 978-1-68119-929-0 (paperback) • ISBN 978-1-68119-930-6 (hardcover)
ISBN 978-1-68119-931-3 (e-book)
Subjects: | CYAC: Unicorns—Fiction. | Princesses—Fiction. | Magic—Fiction. |
Sleepovers—Fiction. | Flight—Fiction. | Fantasy.
Classification: LCC PZ7.1.B633 Fe 2018 (print) | LCC PZ7.1.B633 (e-book) |
DDC [Fic]—dc23
LC record available at https://lccn.loc.gov/2018005074

Book design by Jessie Gang and John Candell
Typeset by Westchester Publishing Services
Printed and bound in the U.S.A. by Berryville Graphics Inc., Berryville, Virginia
4 6 8 10 9 7 5 (paperback)
2 4 6 8 10 9 7 5 3 1 (hardcover)

All papers used by Bloomsbury Publishing, Inc., are natural, recyclable products
made from wood grown in well-managed forests. The manufacturing processes
conform to the environmental regulations of the country of origin.

To find out more about our authors and books visit www.bloomsbury.com
and sign up for our newsletters.

For Phoenix and Lynx

Unicorn Princesses

FEATHER'S FLIGHT

Chapter One

In the top tower of Spiral Palace, Ernest, a wizard-lizard, stood in front of a full-length mirror. He straightened his pointy wizard's hat and furrowed his brow. He pushed his mouth into a straight line. And then he held up his wand as though he were about to cast a spell.

He froze and studied his reflection.

Then, he shook his head. "No, no, no," he whispered. "I look too serious."

He tilted his hat slightly. He widened his eyes and opened his mouth as though he were shouting. He lifted his wand. He paused for a few seconds, and then he sighed. "That's no good, either," he muttered. "I look too . . . enthusiastic."

Ernest began to push his hat backward when he heard a knock on the door. He jumped in surprise and called out, "Come in!"

The door opened with a creak. And there stood a unicorn with a glossy pink coat, a shiny pink mane, and a long pink tail. Around her neck, a ruby hung on a white ribbon necklace.

2

"Princess Feather!" Ernest exclaimed, dancing across the room. "You're back! What a wonderful surprise!"

Feather grinned. "Am I interrupting anything?" she asked.

"Oh no," Ernest said, straightening his cloak. "I was just, um, practicing different poses for casting spells."

Feather laughed. "I just returned from an amazing adventure in the Aqua Realm, the Witches' Realm, and the Reptile Realm. You are one of the first creatures in the Rainbow Realm I wanted to see."

"I've missed you," Ernest said.

"I've missed you too," Feather said. "In the Reptile Realm, I met some wizard-lizards who said you might be their distant cousin. And that made me miss you even more."

Ernest blushed. Then he smiled hopefully. "Now that you're back, you don't happen to need any magical assistance, do you?" he asked. "I've been practicing my magic while you were gone, and now I never make mistakes. Well, hardly ever. Actually, maybe occasionally. But really, I've gotten much better at it."

Feather laughed. "I'm sure you have," she said. "It just so happens that I was wondering if you could make each of my sisters a pair of magic flying pajamas. I'm celebrating my return home with a sleepover in the Sky Castle tonight, and I want to give my sisters a special surprise when they arrive."

Ernest scratched his forehead. "That's a tricky one, even for a wizard-lizard," he said. Then he jumped up. "Actually, I know just the spell! The pajamas will only work for a few hours. And they'll only work in the Rainbow Realm. But I know I can do it! I'll have the magic pajamas waiting for you in the Sky Castle by this afternoon."

"Thanks, Ernest," Feather said. She glanced at the grandfather clock on the other side of the room. "I hate to say this, but I'd better run. My sisters promised to tell me about their new friend while we eat lunch. They say she's a human girl!"

6

Ernest smiled. "That must be Cressida," he said. "You're going to love her. I'll get right to work on those pajamas."

"Thanks, Ernest!" Feather said. "You're the best!" She turned and trotted out the door.

Ernest skipped over to his bookshelf and pulled down a green book with the title *Enchanting Entertaining: From Bewitching Balls to Spellbinding Sleepovers*. He flipped to a chapter in the middle of the book with the heading, "Sorcery for Slumber Parties." He turned more pages until he found a spell with the title, "Short-Lasting Magic Pajamas (Intermediate Level)." He read the spell several times and pulled out his wand. He cleared his throat. And then he chanted, "Dappledy Doopledy Doppledy Damas! Make Seven Pairs of Magic Iguanas!"

Ernest waited for a swirl of wind or a flash of light. He waited for seven pairs of unicorn pajamas to appear on his desktop. Instead thunder rumbled in the distance. "Oh dear!" Ernest said, turning toward the window in time to see a flash of purple light in a distant cluster of pink clouds. "Hopefully Feather won't notice anything amiss before her sleepover," he said. "I'd better try again."

He looked again at his spell book. Then he raised his wand and chanted, "Dappledy Doopledy Doppledy Damas! Make Seven Pairs of Magic Pajamas!"

Pink light flashed. A silvery gust of wind swirled in circles. And then, on his desk, appeared a large brown paper bag. Ernest stood on his tiptoes and peered inside. "Perfecto!" he said. "I knew I could do it." He raised his wand and chanted, "Flippity Flappety Floppety Flastle! Off You Fly to Feather's Sky Castle!"

Two red, glittery wings sprouted on either side of the bag. It took one little hop, flapped its wings, and soared out the window toward the far-off pink clouds.

Chapter Two

On a Saturday afternoon, Cressida Jenkins sat at her kitchen table and used a spoon to put globs of chocolate chip cookie dough on a baking sheet. Her mother stood at the counter chopping carrots while her father stirred a pot of spaghetti sauce.

Cressida was so excited she could barely keep from doing cartwheels across the

kitchen floor. That evening, her two best friends, Gillian and Eleanor, were coming over for dinner and spending the night. It would be their first sleepover, and Cressida was making cookies in honor of the occasion.

Cressida scraped the last bits of dough from the mixing bowl and dropped a final glob onto the only empty spot left on the baking sheet. "These are all ready," Cressida said.

"Excellent," her father said, picking up the baking sheet. "I'll put them right in the oven. You girls can eat cookies in your bedroom together as a special treat."

Cressida grinned. Usually, she wasn't allowed to eat dessert in her bedroom.

"Can we eat dessert before dinner?" Cressida asked.

"We'll see," her mother said, winking at her.

"What else should I do to get ready for Gillian and Eleanor?" Cressida asked. She hopped up and down and spun in circles as she imagined her friends arriving in just fifteen minutes with their sleeping bags and pajamas.

Cressida's father smiled. "It might be a good idea to change your shirt." Cressida looked down at her green T-shirt. Smeared butter covered her sleeves, and there was so much flour on the front that it looked white instead of green.

Cressida smiled. "I guess I got a little

messy when I was making the dough," she said. She skipped across the kitchen, down the hall, and into her bedroom.

She opened her bureau drawer and chose a bright pink shirt with glittery silver and white feathers printed all over it. She pulled off her T-shirt and tossed it in the hamper. As she tugged her pink shirt over her head, she heard a high, tinkling noise. Cressida's heart raced as she pushed her arms through the sleeves. She leaped over to her bedside table, opened the drawer, and wrapped her fingers around an old-fashioned key with a crystal-ball handle that was glowing bright pink. The key had been a gift from her friends, the unicorn princesses. Whenever they wanted to invite her to visit them in their magical world, the Rainbow Realm, they made the key's handle glow and pulse.

Cressida glanced at the unicorn clock on her bedroom wall. Gillian and Eleanor would be arriving in 11 minutes. Fortunately, time in the human world froze while Cressida was in the Rainbow Realm, meaning that even if she spent hours with the unicorn princesses, she could still return in time to greet Gillian and Eleanor at her front door. Cressida wasn't sure if she was more excited to visit the Rainbow Realm or to have her first sleepover, and she was glad she didn't have to choose between the two.

Cressida pushed the key into the back

15

pocket of her jeans. She pulled her silver unicorn sneakers from the bottom of her closet and put them on. And then she ran down the hall, through the living room, and toward the back door.

"Cressida?" her mother said. "Are you going outside? Aren't your friends about to come over?"

"I'll be back in five minutes," Cressida called out. She dashed out the door, across her backyard, and through the woods behind her house until she came to a giant oak tree. She kneeled and pushed her magic key into a tiny hole in the tree's base. Immediately, the forest began to spin. First, it was a blur of brown tree trunks, green leaves, and blue sky. Then everything went pitch black, and Cressida felt as though she were falling fast through space. Just when she started to feel nervous that she had been falling for too long, she landed gently on something soft.

The darkness lifted, and for a few seconds all Cressida could see was a swirl of white, pink, and purple. But soon enough, the spinning slowed to a stop. Cressida blinked and looked around her. She knew exactly where she was: sitting on an enormous lavender velvet sofa in the front hall of Spiral Palace, the unicorn princesses' horn-shaped home.

Chapter Three

Cressida blinked when she looked across the room and counted not seven, but eight—eight!—unicorns eating roinkleberries and froyananas from silver troughs. The unicorns she already knew and loved were there—yellow Princess Sunbeam, silver Princess Flash, green Princess Bloom, purple Princess Prism, blue Princess Breeze, black

Princess Moon, and orange Princess Firefly. There was also a pink unicorn Cressida had never met. The unicorns were so absorbed in their conversation that they didn't notice Cressida's arrival.

"And then," Bloom said to her sisters between bites of froyanana, "there were quail everywhere. They were eating all the cake and ice cream, and they were playing with all the decorations. I was sure my birthday garden ball was ruined. But Cressida saved the day! She organized a surprise birthday party in the palace."

"Wow," the pink unicorn said. "She sounds amazing."

"She definitely is," Moon said. "She built a new ballroom in the Night Forest when

Ernest cast a spell that made the old one disappear."

"And she found my magic yellow sapphire in a cactus flower," Sunbeam said.

"She even saved the Thunder Dash course from a flood of cake batter," Flash said.

"If it weren't for her, there would still be giant bats sleeping on the kites we use for the Blast," Breeze said.

"And I would still be crystal clear instead of purple," Prism said. "I couldn't believe it when she found the Valley of Light's missing rainbow."

"We wouldn't even have a library if she hadn't come to the rescue," Firefly said.

"I can't wait to meet Cressida," the pink

unicorn said. "Do you think she'll get here soon?"

Cressida smiled, stood up, and said, "Hello!"

The unicorns turned toward her.

"My human girl is back!" Sunbeam sang as she danced over to Cressida.

"Welcome to your home away from home!" said Flash, rearing up and galloping over.

"We're so glad you could come," said Bloom and Prism as they trotted toward Cressida.

Breeze and Moon grinned, swished their tails, and said, "Hello!"

"Cressida, there's someone we can't wait for you to meet," Firefly said, jumping

21

with excitement. "Do you remember, during your last visit to the Rainbow Realm, when I told you we have another sister? Here she is! She just got back from a big trip. We've been telling her about you all afternoon, and she was so excited to meet you that she insisted we invite you here right away."

"It's wonderful to meet you," Cressida said.

"My sisters have been talking about you nonstop," the pink unicorn said. "I'm Princess Feather. After my sisters told me all about you, I wanted to invite you to my sleepover tonight. Would you like to join us? I'm hosting it in my domain, the Sky Castle."

"I'd love to," Cressida said, thinking

she was awfully lucky to go to two sleepovers in one night.

"Fantastic!" Feather said. Her ruby glittered, pink sparkling light poured from her horn, and she flew straight up into the air and did a somersault. "I'm so excited I can't stay on the ground," she said, giggling and doing figure eights around the chandeliers.

Sunbeam, Flash, Bloom, Prism, Breeze, Moon, and Firefly laughed.

"The palace sure has seemed empty without Feather flying all over the place," Bloom said.

"I've even missed the sound of her hooves crashing into the chandeliers," Flash said.

For a few seconds, Feather's sisters grinned. Then Prism sighed, and her smile faded. "I just wish we could go with you on some of your trips," she said to Feather.

"Me, too," Moon said.

"We never get to go anywhere," Flash said.

"It's not fair," Sunbeam said.

"I wouldn't want to travel as much as Feather does," Firefly said. "But I'd love it if all eight of us could leave the Realm together occasionally."

Bloom nodded and frowned.

"Why can't you all go on an adventure together?" Cressida asked.

"The only way we know of to travel to

far-off realms is to fly extremely fast," Flash explained. "Feather is the only one of us with that magic power."

"The only exception is the human world," Breeze said. "The keys we have are a magic short cut. But we only have two—the one you have, and the one we have. So we can't even all travel to the human world together."

"It's really disappointing," Moon said, sighing.

Feather landed on the marble floor. "I'm so sorry you feel left out," she said. "I wish I could somehow take you with me. I really do."

The other unicorns nodded.

"We know you don't mean to exclude us," Sunbeam said, trying to smile.

Feather took a deep breath. "I was planning to show you all my pictures and souvenirs at the sleepover tonight. Do you still want to see them? I'm so very excited to show them to you and to tell you about my adventures. I even have a special surprise gift for you. But I don't want to leave you feeling even worse." She smiled hopefully.

"Of course we want to see them," Bloom said.

The other unicorns nodded and smiled. But Cressida could see in their faces that they all felt at least a little jealous.

"Great," Feather said, sounding relieved.

She turned to Cressida. "How would you like to come with me to the Sky Castle to help me get ready?"

"I'd love that!" Cressida said.

Feather kneeled so Cressida could climb onto her back. But just then, a high, nasal voice—a voice that could only be Ernest's—called out, "Just a minute! Don't leave yet!" A few seconds later, Ernest sprinted into the front hall.

"Hello, Ernest!" Cressida said, laughing.

"Before you go, I have just the thing for you," Ernest said. "I've been practicing this spell all afternoon, and I've most certainly got it!"

Cressida giggled and braced herself for a magical mishap.

Ernest pulled his wand from his cloak pocket, held it up, and chanted, "Fairily Merrily Flippity Flings! Please Make Cressida a Pair of Kings!"

Wind swirled around Cressida. Red light flashed. And then two men wearing furry red robes and gold crowns appeared. Each sat on a purple throne and held a scepter covered in rubies and emeralds.

"You must bow and curtsy!" one bellowed.

"And call me 'Your Highness!'" the other demanded.

"Oh dear!" Ernest said, rolling his eyes. "I thought I'd ironed out that wrinkle. I've had kings trying to order me around all afternoon. Just ignore them." Ernest held up his wand and chanted, "Royalty Spoilty Clappity Clings! Please Send Away these Two Cranky Kings! Now Make Cressida a Pair of Wings!"

More wind circled around Cressida. Pink light flashed. The kings vanished,

and Cressida felt something light on her back, between her shoulders. She reached behind her and felt two large, filmy wings.

Cressida grinned. Ever since she had been a little girl, she had wanted to have wings, just like a fairy. And now she did! "Thank you, Ernest!" she said. "How do they work?"

Ernest blushed. "I haven't the faintest idea," he said. "You'll have to ask Feather." He pulled a watch on a long chain from his cloak pocket. "Well, look at the time. I'm afraid I'd better get going!" And with that, he sprinted off down the hall.

"I can teach you how to fly," Feather said, winking at Cressida. She kneeled again. "But for now, why don't you ride on my back? It's a long flight to the Sky Castle, especially for a beginner."

Cressida climbed onto Feather and gripped the unicorn's shiny mane.

Feather looked at her sisters. "I'll send a cloud down to pick you up as soon as we get to the Sky Castle."

"See you soon!" Sunbeam called as Feather trotted across the front hall and out the palace door.

Chapter Four

Feather trotted along the clear stones that led from Spiral Palace to the surrounding forest. She began to gallop. Pink glittery light poured from her horn, and Feather and Cressida soared up into the air.

"Whoa," Cressida laughed, leaning forward and wrapping her arms around Feather's neck.

"The only way to get to the Sky Castle is to fly or take a cloud," Feather said. "And honestly, the clouds are too slow for my taste. If there's one thing I love, it's flying fast!"

Feather rocketed through the sky. Wind riffled through Cressida's hair and battered the bare skin on her face and hands. After several minutes, Feather swooped down and landed on a giant pink cloud covered in cotton candy–colored mist. "We're here!" Feather said, kneeling.

Cressida slid off her back. To her delight, the cloud felt soft and springy under her feet, like a cross between a mattress and a trampoline. She hopped back and forth and giggled. Feather laughed and jumped from side to side.

"This is really fun," Feather said, "but flying is even better. You're going to love it. And I can't wait to teach you!"

"I can't wait to learn," Cressida said, touching the two wings on her back to make sure they were still there.

"We just need a little help from a cloud," Feather said. "And that reminds me—we need to send one down to get my sisters."

Feather whistled, and two clouds that were as big as Cressida's bedroom rug turned and floated toward them. Each one had round teal eyes, a cauliflower nose, and a grinning mouth.

"Hello, Princess Feather," one of the clouds said.

"Welcome back," the other said.

Feather smiled. "This is my new friend, Cressida Jenkins." Then, she looked at Cressida. "And these are my cloud friends, Cleo and Cloe."

"It's a pleasure to meet you," Cressida said.

"It's lovely to meet you, too," Cleo and Cloe said.

"Cleo," Feather said, "is there any chance you might be free to go pick up my sisters? We're having a sleepover tonight."

"Absolutely!" Cleo said, bobbing up and down with excitement. "I love any excuse I can find to drift down to Spiral Palace! And unicorn princesses are my very favorite passengers!" Cleo hummed as she turned and floated away.

"Thank you," Feather said. Then she looked at Cloe. "I'm about to give Cressida her very first flying lesson. Would you like to join us?"

"Definitely!" Cloe said. "How can I help?"

"I wonder if you could float under her while she's getting started," Feather said. "That way, if she falls, you can catch her."

"Sure thing!" Cloe said.

Feather looked at Cressida and grinned. "Are you ready?"

Cressida's heart pounded with excitement. "I can't wait!" she said.

"The first thing to do," Feather said, grinning, "is close your eyes and imagine lifting up into the air."

Cressida closed her eyes. She visualized herself rising upward, above the clouds and mist. But she couldn't feel anything happening. After several seconds, Cressida said, "It's not working." Her heart sank. What if she couldn't fly after all?

Feather and Cloe giggled.

"Open your eyes!" Feather called out.

Cressida opened her eyes to discover she was hovering in the air, twenty feet above where Feather stood. Cloe was right under Cressida, grinning.

"You're a natural," Cloe said.

Cressida laughed.

Feather's ruby sparkled. Glittery pink light poured from her horn. And then she flew into the air and joined Cressida. "I

can't believe you did it on your first try,"
Feather said. "Shall we try flying forward
and backward?"

"Sure!" Cressida said. She imagined

herself speeding forward, and, to her delight, she shot out ahead of Feather. "Whee!" she cried. She stopped and imagined flying in reverse. She bolted backward.

"I can barely keep up!" Cloe said, laughing.

"You didn't need me to teach you anything!" Feather said. "Want to do some tricks?"

"Definitely," Cressida said.

"I'll be right here in case you need me," Cloe said, floating under Feather and Cressida.

"Watch this," Feather said. She flew straight upward, stopped for half a second, and did three somersaults.

"My turn!" Cressida said. She sped

upward, paused, and then imagined herself somersaulting. Instantly, she found herself laughing as she tumbled in the air.

"Now, let's try doing some loops," Feather said as she began to fly in a giant circle. Cressida watched her for a few seconds and then joined her. Soon Cressida and Feather were flying in faster and faster loops.

"I'm starting to get dizzy," Feather said, slowing down.

Cressida giggled. "Me too," she said.

"I'm getting dizzy just watching you!" Cloe called out. "This is the closest a cloud can get to doing a somersault," she added, laughing as she spun in a circle.

"Not bad!" Feather said. Then, she looked at Cressida. "I could do this all day, but I think we'd better head over to the Sky Castle to get ready for the sleepover. But would you like to do something fun on our way back down?"

"Sure!" Cressida said.

"Oh, I bet I know what you're thinking, Feather," Cloe said, laughing. She floated so she was right under Feather and Cressida. "I'm ready when you are."

Feather looked at Cressida. "Imagine you're not flying anymore," she said, with a playful smile.

"Really?" Cressida asked. "But won't I fall?"

"Don't worry," Feather said, winking. "Cloe will catch us. And she's the softest cloud I know."

Cressida took a deep breath. She imagined she was no longer flying. Suddenly she and Feather plummeted down and landed on Cloe. Sure enough, Cloe felt like one giant soft, fluffy pillow. Cressida laughed. "That was almost as much fun as flying!" she said.

Feather smiled. "I agree!" she said. "Thanks so much for catching us, Cloe."

"My pleasure," the cloud said. "And now that you're my passengers, shall I take you to the Sky Castle?"

"Yes, please," Feather said.

"Here we go," Cloe said. She made a sharp turn to the right and floated through a patch of mist so thick and pink that Cressida couldn't see anything. After several seconds, they came out the other side, and right in front of them was a sparkling palace made of giant rubies and pale pink pearls. Two feather-shaped turrets reached up into the sky, and a fuchsia flag with a giant white feather on it hung over the magenta front door.

"What a beautiful castle," Cressida said.

"It's a lot smaller than Spiral Palace," Feather said. "But it's the perfect place for a sleepover."

Cloe stopped in front of the door, and Feather and Cressida slid off her.

"Thanks so much for the ride," Feather said.

"And thank you for your help during the flying lesson," Cressida said.

"My pleasure!" Cloe said. "I hope you have a great sleepover."

Cloe winked, turned, and drifted away.

"I can't wait to show you the inside," Feather said. She used her mouth to open the front door, and she and Cressida stepped into a grand foyer. Gleaming rose-colored tiles covered the floor. Chandeliers made of pearls and rubies hung from the ceiling. Threads of mist floated in through the windows. On the floor was a large brown paper bag with red, glittery wings.

Feather peeked into the bag and smiled. "I asked Ernest to make my sisters magic pajamas that will allow them to fly for a few hours, and it looks like they made it here safe and sound!" Her eyes widened, and she grinned. "Let's go see the Adventure Room!"

Chapter Five

Cressida followed Feather down a hallway made of shiny coral- and rose-colored stones. They turned left, through a pearl and ruby archway, and into a room with more pictures hanging on the walls and more shelves crammed with interesting objects than Cressida had ever seen. In the far corner of the room, next to an open window, was a magenta armchair.

Feather danced over to a wall covered in pictures. "Want to see the pictures from my most recent adventure? I just hung them up this morning. I can't wait to show you and my sisters!"

"Definitely," Cressida said, grinning as she rushed over to Feather.

"These are from the Aqua Realm," Feather explained, nodding to the pictures of her with some mermaids, drinking a bottle of green liquid as they lounged on a rocky shore, swimming with rainbow-striped dolphins in a shallow cove, and wearing an air bubble over her head as she

danced with an octopus. "That green stuff is seaweed juice," Feather explained, wrinkling her nose. "It tasted absolutely terrible, but I pretended to like it."

Cressida grimaced. "It was probably very healthy," she said.

Feather laughed. "I bet you're right! I still have the bottle. It's on that shelf right below us."

Cressida looked down and saw a glass bottle covered in a seashell design. Next to it on the shelf sat a red flute and silver cauldron.

"These are my pictures from the Reptile Realm," Feather continued, pointing with her hoof to images of her flying with winged orange turtles, hopping with red

51

frogs, and sunbathing with more purple iguanas than Cressida could count. "That red flute was a gift from the frogs. They told me it's magic, but to be honest, it's hard to play a flute if you have hooves."

Cressida giggled.

"And here are my pictures from the Witches' Realm," Feather said, glancing at two pictures of her hiking up a mountain with silver witches wearing tall black hats and bulging backpacks. "They gave me that cauldron as a souvenir. I've always wanted to make a magic potion."

"Me too," Cressida said.

Feather laughed. "Maybe someday we can make one together!"

Cressida looked at the pictures for

several more seconds. "I love seeing these," she said. "But I have a question. Do unicorns have cameras?"

"What's a camera?" Feather said, looking curious.

"It's something humans use to take photographs," Cressida said.

"I'll have to put that on my list of things to see if I ever get to visit the human world," Feather said. "No, unicorns don't have cameras. I made these with the help of the Imagibirds." Feather smiled. "Would you like to give it a try?"

"Sure," Cressida said.

Feather turned toward the magenta armchair. "Have a seat right there, close your eyes, and think of a happy memory."

53

"Okay!" Cressida said. She climbed onto the chair. At first, her mind was blank. And then she remembered the moment she had found Sunbeam's yellow sapphire and put it back on the yellow unicorn's ribbon necklace during her first visit to the Rainbow Realm. Immediately, Cressida heard chirping. Then four small pink birds fluttered in through the window carrying in their talons a small, square picture on a thick piece of paper.

54

"Thank you," Cressida said, as she took it from the birds.

"Our pleasure!" chirped the birds, and they flew back out the window.

Cressida stared at the paper. There she was, standing next to an ecstatic Sunbeam with a shimmering yellow sapphire hanging around her neck. The cacti and the dunes grinned with relief. And the purple sand shimmered and glittered in the sunlight. "Wow," Cressida said. "That's amazing!"

"Do you want more?" Feather asked. "I know from my sisters you've been on quite a few adventures here."

"I'd love that," Cressida said. Next, she remembered crossing the finish line when she ran in the Thunder Dash. Immediately,

55

the Imagibirds fluttered in carrying a picture of her sprinting on the crushed diamond race course, with Flash cheering her on. She made a few more pictures with the help of the Imagibirds: there was one of her grimacing as she tried a froyanana in the Enchanted Garden with Bloom, one of her and Prism painting the rainbow-colored grass in the Valley of Light, one of her and Breeze making an octopus together with metamorflower petals, one of her dancing with Moon while a raccoon played a flarpophone, and one of her casting a spell with Firefly as she gripped a magic stalactite in the Shimmering Caves.

When Cressida finished, Feather looked at the images. "Those are lovely," she said.

"Why don't you put them right by the glass bottle I got from the mermaids?" Feather nodded to an empty spot on the shelf of souvenirs. "You can get them before you leave."

"Thanks so much," Cressida said.

"No problem," Feather said. "And I think now we'd better go get the Great Hall ready for the sleepover."

Cressida followed Feather out of the Adventure Room and farther down the hallway, toward a white door decorated with pearls arranged in the shape of a feather. As they walked, Cressida heard what sounded like soft whimpering.

"What's that noise?" Feather asked, looking worried.

The noise got louder as they got closer to the door. "Oh dear," Feather said. "After all the stories from my sisters about Ernest's magical mishaps, I'm afraid to look." Feather winced and used her mouth to pull the door open. Immediately, she gasped and said, "Oh no!"

Chapter Six

Cressida looked through the doorway and into a grand room with high coral-colored ceilings and tall windows. Inside, she counted fourteen giant purple iguanas curled up in pairs, shivering, and crying. There were iguanas huddled together on salmon-colored velvet sofas. There were iguanas sniffling on a white, feather-shaped rug. And there were

iguanas staring longingly out the windows. As Cressida looked more closely at the iguanas, she noticed they looked exactly like the ones in the pictures of Feather's trip to the Reptile Realm.

The iguanas turned and looked at Cressida and Feather. Tears ran down their scaly cheeks. And then one called out, "Is that you, Princess Feather?" He got up from the rug and crept toward her.

Cressida took a step backward, feeling wary of the huge reptile. But Feather galloped toward the iguana. "Ivan!" she exclaimed. "What in the world are you doing here?"

"I'm so relieved to see you," Ivan said, smiling even though his teeth were

61

chattering. "We were having a perfectly nice time dozing on tree branches and rocks in the afternoon sun. And then, out of nowhere, wind swirled all around us, there was a flash of light, and we were suddenly here in this room."

"We've never been so cold and scared," another iguana said.

"All we want to do is go home," said another.

"I'm almost positive we're in the Arctic Realm," another said. "It's freezing!"

Feather smiled sympathetically. "I can assure you you're in the Rainbow Realm. But I know it's much colder than in the Reptile Realm. Especially up here in the Sky Castle."

62

"As glad as I am to see you, do you think you could magically transport us home as soon as possible?" Ivan asked. "We're really miserable."

"Of course," Feather said. "I'm so sorry this happened to you, and I promise to get you back to the Reptile Realm this afternoon." She turned toward Cressida. "These are my dear friends, the iguanas." Then she turned to the iguanas. "And this is my friend Cressida."

"It's a pleasure to meet you," Cressida said. "And I'm sorry you're so cold and unhappy. I'll do everything I can to help Feather."

The iguanas, who had mostly stopped crying, nodded. "Thank you," Ivan said.

63

"If anyone can help us, it's Princess Feather," another iguana said.

Feather smiled reassuringly at the iguanas. Then, she turned to Cressida with wide eyes and whispered, "What on earth will we do?"

"Is there anything here we could use to help the iguanas warm up while we try to think of a plan?" Cressida asked.

"Good idea," Feather said to Cressida. She galloped over to a shelf and pulled down a pile of pink and red velvet sleeping bags. Cressida quickly draped the sleeping bags over the iguanas.

"Thank you," Ivan said. "That helps."

"Cressida and I are about to come up

72

with a plan," Feather said. Then, in an anxious voice, she whispered to Cressida, "Do you have any ideas yet? I feel so worried and upset that I can't think of anything. What if the iguanas are stuck here forever?"

"I can completely understand how you feel," Cressida whispered. She knew that feeling panicked and anxious usually made it almost impossible to come up with creative ways to solve problems. She took a deep breath and looked at the iguanas. "You don't happen to have any magic powers, do you?" she asked, hoping the iguanas might be able to fly.

Ivan sighed and shivered. "Our only

magic power is to turn flowers into cupcakes. Which is only useful if you're outside in a meadow and want dessert."

"I see," Cressida said, trying not to giggle.

"Do you have magic powers?" Ivan asked.

Cressida opened her mouth to say no. But then she paused. That wasn't exactly true: the last time she had been to the Rainbow Realm she had used a spell book to cast a spell. And as she remembered the spell book, she wondered if it just might come in handy again. "I'm not usually magic," Cressida said with a smile. "But occasionally I am."

Cressida turned to Feather. "I have an

idea," she said. "The last time I visited the Rainbow Realm, I had a spell book that's still in the Glow Library in the Magic section. Do you think there's any chance we could go get it?"

"The Shimmering Caves are all the way on the other side of the Rainbow Realm," Feather said, looking unsure. Then, her face brightened. "I know how we could fly there quickly! Why don't you ride on my back and fly at the same time? Then we'll go twice as fast."

"Good idea!" Cressida said. Feather kneeled, and Cressida climbed onto her back.

"We'll be right back," Feather assured the iguanas. Then, she turned and galloped down the hall, and out the front door. Once they were outside, pink glittery light poured from Feather's horn, and she and Cressida lifted into the air.

"Start flying at the count of three," Feather called out. "One. Two. Three!"

Cressida imagined herself speeding

68

forward, and suddenly she and Feather were hurtling through the sky.

After a few minutes, Feather said, "We're almost there. You can stop flying, and I'll take it from here."

Cressida imagined stopping as Feather landed with a jolt right in front of an orange door in the side of a rocky hill. Cressida recognized it as the entrance to the Shimmering Caves. "That was the very fastest I've ever gone," Feather said.

"It was pretty fun," Cressida said, giggling.

"And now, I'm thrilled to sneak a peek at the Glow Library," Feather said. "I was disappointed to miss the opening."

Feather pulled open the door, and with Cressida still on her back, she galloped along a corridor, down a spiral staircase, along another hallway, and right up to a door with a sign above it that read, in orange gemstones, "WELCOME TO THE GLOW LIBRARY." She kneeled, and Cressida slid off her back. Feather pulled opened the door, and for a few seconds she and Cressida admired the library. Firefly-shaped chandeliers hung from the ceiling, reading lights brimmed with fireflies, gigantic reading chairs sat in every nook and cranny, and floor-to-ceiling shelves held hundreds of books—even more books than had been there when Cressida last visited. Three fairies stood together in front of the Art and Artists section, and a dragon was browsing a new section labeled, "Cooking."

"What an amazing library," Feather said. "I'll have to check out the Adventure section soon. Do you know where your book is?"

"I think so," Cressida said, and she walked over to the Magic section. She read the titles on the spines of the books—*Planting Magic Flowers in Five Easy Steps*, *Magic Wands: A Complete Guide*, *Unicorn Horn Care and Maintenance*, and *Top Spells for Gnomes*—until she came to exactly the one she wanted: *Spells for Human Girls and Boys*.

Cressida pulled the book off the shelf and quickly turned to the table of contents.

She read through the list of spells, smiling when she came to the one titled, "Returning Characters to Books." She felt relieved and excited when she read the title of the very last spell in the book: "Traveling from One Realm to Another (Very Advanced)." Cressida grinned and bounded back to Feather.

"This book has just the spell we need," Cressida said as she climbed onto Feather's back. She tucked the book under her arm and grabbed Feather's mane.

"Fantastic!" Feather said. She pulled open the library door and galloped through the Shimmering Caves and back out into the sunlight. "Let's fly back at the count of three," Feather said. "One. Two.

Three!" Pink glittery light streamed from Feather's horn, and she soared up into the sky as Cressida imagined flying as fast as she possibly could. Soon, they were rocketing through the air at lightning speed. After a few minutes, Feather said, "We're here. You can stop flying now." Cressida and Feather slowed down and landed right outside the Sky Castle.

"Phew," Feather said. "That was exhausting and wonderful all at the same time!"

"I agree!" Cressida said. She felt tired and exhilarated in just the same way she had after the Thunder Dash.

Feather kneeled down, and Cressida slid off her back. She sat down on the Sky

Castle's front step, flipped to the last page of the book, and began to read:

Traveling from One Realm to Another
(Very Advanced)

INGREDIENTS:

Magic cauldron

Magic flute

Purple sand

Diamond gravel

Froyananas

Rainbow grass

Metamorflower petals

Flarpophone strings

Stalactite dust

Picture of the destination

METHOD:

Combine the sand, gravel, froyananas, grass, petals, strings, and dust in the cauldron. Cover the cauldron, and play the magic flute for several seconds. When the cauldron begins to hum, stop playing and lift the cauldron lid. The potion inside should be bubbling, but it won't be hot. Sprinkle the potion on everyone who wants to travel and the picture of the desired destination.

Cressida read through the instructions three times. She looked up to ask Feather how they might get all the ingredients. But before she could speak, she spotted

Sunbeam, Flash, Bloom, Prism, Breeze, Moon, and Firefly leaping off Cleo and trotting toward the Sky Castle.

"Hello!" Sunbeam said.

"That was the longest cloud ride ever," Prism said, rolling her eyes and smiling.

"It was so bumpy that I feel a little sick," Bloom said, looking a little greener than usual.

"What are you reading?" Firefly asked. "Isn't that a library book?"

"And why are you sitting out here?" Moon asked.

"Are we still having a sleepover?" Flash asked.

"I sure hope so," Feather said. She

quickly told her sisters all about the cold, miserable iguanas waiting to go home.

"You can't say we didn't warn you about Ernest's magical mishaps," Breeze said.

"How are we going to get the iguanas home?" Prism asked.

"What if they're stuck here forever?" Flash asked.

"I have a plan," Cressida said. "But first, Sunbeam, do you think you could make the sun over the Sky Castle just as warm as it is in the Glitter Canyon? That would make the iguanas comfortable while they're waiting."

"Sure thing!" Sunbeam said. Her yellow sapphire sparkled, and light poured from her horn. Suddenly, the sun shone much brighter, and Cressida felt like she was outside on a perfectly warm summer afternoon. Cressida heard cheering noises coming from the Sky Castle, and a voice that sounded like Ivan's shouted, "Thank you!"

"Next," Cressida said, "I'm going to need help from all of you. We need the ingredients on this page." She held up the book while the unicorns studied it.

"I'd be glad to go get some purple sand from the Glitter Canyon," Sunbeam said.

"I'll get the diamond gravel from the race course back in the Thunder Peaks," Flash said.

78

"I have some froyananas that are ripe back in the Enchanted Garden," Bloom said.

"And I could get some rainbow grass from the Valley of Light," Prism added.

"I'm sure the Night Forest raccoons would give me some strings from one of their flarpophones," Moon said.

"I could get some metamorflower petals from the Windy Meadows," Breeze said.

"And I can get the stalactite dust from the Shimmering Caves," Firefly said.

"Let's go!" Sunbeam said, starting to turn and gallop. But then she halted and the look of excitement vanished from her face. "It's going to take us forever to travel by cloud all the way back to our domains."

"It will take hours and hours," Bloom said, grimacing.

"We'll have to cancel the sleepover," Feather said, as her eyes filled with tears.

Cressida put her hand on Feather to comfort her. And then she paused. Cressida leaned over to Feather and whispered, "Do you think this would be a good time to give your sisters their magic pajamas? Then they could fly to their domains, get the ingredients, and come back!"

Feather's eyes lit up and she smiled. "Excellent idea!" she said. She turned to her sisters. "Wait here for just a second! I have a gift for you!"

Chapter Seven

Feather opened the Sky Castle door, disappeared for a few seconds, and returned holding the brown paper bag in her mouth.

Cressida grinned: She wanted to see what, exactly, unicorns wore to bed.

Feather dropped the bag on the front step of the castle and used her mouth to pull out a pink fleece one-piece suit with four legs, a zipper up the front, and a hole for a tail. Cressida giggled. It reminded her of the pajamas she wore to bed when she was a baby. She brought the pajamas over to Sunbeam and helped her step into them. Then, she zipped them up.

"Thanks so much for the pajamas," Sunbeam said. "But why are we getting ready for bed now? Don't we need to help the iguanas?"

"You'll see," Feather said, winking.

Feather pulled out another pair, and Cressida helped Flash put them on. Then, she helped Bloom, Prism, Breeze, Moon, and Firefly. Cressida giggled at the sight of seven unicorns wearing pink pajamas.

"These are such a thoughtful gift,"

Prism said. "But will you please tell us why we're getting dressed for bed? The sun hasn't even set!"

"See what happens if you gallop and then jump," Feather said with a grin.

Sunbeam, Flash, Bloom, Prism, Breeze, Moon, and Firefly looked at each other and shrugged. Then, they all began to gallop.

"One. Two. Three!" Flash called out, and they all leaped into the air. Instead of landing after a second or two, they all soared upward.

"Whoa!" Sunbeam called out. "This is so much fun!"

"This is even better than running," Flash said.

"This is amazing!" Prism said, doing a somersault.

"I get it!" Bloom said. "Now we can fly to our domains and get the ingredients we need super quickly."

"We'll be back as soon as possible," Breeze said, as she and her sisters flew away.

"Great!" shouted Feather. "We'll meet you in the Great Hall."

Cressida took a deep breath. "Let's go get the magic cauldron, the magic flute, and one of your pictures of the Reptile Realm."

"Good idea," Feather said. Cressida grabbed her spell book, and the two ran back into the castle, down the hall, and into the Adventure Room.

Feather found the picture with her sunbathing with the iguanas, and pulled it down with her mouth. Cressida rushed to the shelf below. She picked up the red flute and tucked it, along with her spell book, under her arm. Then she used both hands to lift the cauldron. "Wow!" Cressida said. "This is really heavy!"

"Tell me about it!" Feather said. "I flew the whole way back from the Witch's Realm with it." Then she smiled nervously and added, "I really do hope this works."

"I think it will," Cressida said. She had to admit, though, that she wasn't entirely sure it would: She had never made a magic potion.

Cressida and Feather walked down the hallway and into the Great Hall. The iguanas smiled hopefully when they saw Cressida and Feather.

"Thank you for making it warmer," Ivan said. "That really helped a lot."

"I'm so glad," Cressida said. "We'll get you home soon." Cressida put the spell book, the flute, and the cauldron on the floor. Then she took the picture from Feather and put it right next to the cauldron.

"I sure hope so," Ivan said.

Cressida heard the clatter of hooves on the hallway's tile floor. The door opened, and in galloped Sunbeam, Flash, Bloom,

Prism, Breeze, Moon, and Firefly, all carrying buckets in their mouths.

"Are you ready?" Cressida asked.

The unicorns nodded.

Cressida opened the spell book to the last page. She took a deep breath. She wasn't sure if she was qualified to do an advanced spell. She had never played a flute, let alone a magic one. And she certainly hadn't ever brewed a potion in a magic cauldron. But, she told herself, there was a first time for everything.

Cressida took the bucket from Sunbeam's mouth. Inside was shimmering purple sand. She emptied the bucket into the cauldron. Next, she poured in the crushed diamond gravel from Flash. Then

she added the froyananas from Bloom, the rainbow grass from Prism, the metamor-flower petals from Breeze, the flarpophone strings from Moon, and the stalactite dust from Firefly. Cressida put the lid on the cauldron.

"Here we go!" Cressida said, smiling nervously at her eight unicorn friends.

"Let's do it!" Feather said.

Cressida picked up the red flute. She took a deep breath, arranged her fingers over the holes, and blew into the mouthpiece. To her astonishment, some of the most beautiful music she had ever heard came out. She lifted her fingers to play different notes. The unicorns closed their eyes and rocked back and forth. The iguanas gathered in a circle around the cauldron. Soon they closed their eyes and began to sway.

After a minute, Cressida heard a soft humming noise that grew louder and louder. She put the flute down and lifted the cauldron lid. Inside, a pink liquid bubbled. "I can't believe that worked," Cressida whispered. She dipped her hand into the liquid and sprinkled it on each of the iguanas' noses.

"That tickles," Ivan said, twitching his nose when the pink droplets fell on him.

Next, Cressida sprinkled the potion on Feather's picture. Wind swirled around the room. A purple light flashed. And the iguanas vanished.

"You did it!" Feather exclaimed.

"Next time you come to the Glow Library, we'll have to get you an advanced spell book," Firefly said, winking.

"Now we can have our sleepover!" Feather said. "Thank you, Cressida! You saved the day!"

"It was my pleasure," Cressida said.

"And now I can show all of you my pictures and souvenirs!" Feather said, hopping back and forth.

Chapter Eight

Feather led Cressida and her unicorn sisters down the hall and into the Adventure Room. Sunbeam, Flash, Bloom, Prism, Breeze, Moon, and Firefly, still wearing their magic pajamas, flew from picture to picture and souvenir to souvenir, asking Feather to tell them stories about her adventures.

After a while, Sunbeam sighed and said,

"You know, I really do love seeing all your pictures, but the more I look at them, the sadder I feel that we can't go on even one of your trips with you."

"Me, too," Flash said. "These are great stories. I'm so glad you're sharing them with us. But now I want to go on an adventure, too."

"I want to go somewhere right now," Breeze said.

Bloom and Prism nodded.

Firefly frowned. "It would be so much fun to see something new," she said.

"I'm sorry you couldn't come with me," Feather said. Her bottom lip quivered, and Cressida could tell she was trying not to cry. "But can't we still have fun together tonight? Especially after all our hard work to help the iguanas."

Cressida looked at Sunbeam, Flash, Bloom, Prism, Breeze, Moon, and Firefly. She could see that they felt awfully left out. And then, Cressida had another idea.

"How would you like to come with me on an adventure right now? My human friends and I were about to have a sleepover at my house when you invited me here. Would you like to join us?"

"Really?" Flash asked, looking excited.

"In the human world?" Prism asked.

"A sleepover with human girls? That sounds amazing!" Moon said.

"But we only have two keys," Firefly said. "Remember?"

Cressida smiled at her friends. "I have a plan," she said, winking. She skipped over to the magenta chair in the corner, by the window. She closed her eyes and remembered what her backyard had looked like just before she left. Soon the Imagibirds flew in through the window with a picture of her green lawn, her swing set, and her family's picnic table.

Next, Cressida ran over to the shelf of souvenirs from Feather's most recent trip. She picked up the bottle from the mermaids and the stack of pictures from her memories of the Rainbow Realm. She slid the pictures into the back pocket of her jeans, so she would be sure not to forget them. "I'll be right back," said, and she raced down the hallway to the Great Hall. She skipped over to the cauldron, unscrewed the bottle top, and dipped the bottle into the pink liquid until it was full. She put the top back on the bottle and returned to the Adventure Room.

"Are you ready to visit the human world for a sleepover?" she asked, grinning.

"Yes!" all the unicorns said at once.

Then Sunbeam blushed and said, "Well, I'm almost ready. Is there any chance you could help me take off my magic pajamas before we go? I'm getting a little hot!"

"Me, too!" Flash and Breeze said.

The other unicorns nodded.

"Sure thing," Cressida said, and she helped each unicorn unzip and step out of her pajamas.

"Now we really are ready!" Firefly said.

"Great!" Cressida said, and she used the bottle to spritz the pink potion on each of the unicorns' heads. She sprinkled a little on herself. And finally, she sprinkled some on the picture of her backyard. She had just enough time to put the top back on the bottle and push it into her pocket when a gust of wind raced around the room. Light flashed. And suddenly, in the time it took Cressida to blink, she and the unicorn princesses were standing in her back yard.

For a few seconds, Sunbeam, Flash, Bloom, Prism, Breeze, Moon, Firefly, and

98

Feather looked all around them with wide eyes. "What in the world is that thing?" Moon asked, using her nose to point to the swing set.

Cressida giggled. "It's something human girls and boys go on to feel like they're flying," she explained.

"Is that your palace?" Bloom asked, looking at Cressida's house.

"It's sort of like a palace," Cressida said, smiling. "Would you like to come inside?"

"Definitely!" Breeze said.

"We'd love to," Flash said.

"I can't wait to see where you live," Feather said.

"Come right this way," Cressida said.

She walked to the back door, and opened it. Her parents were still in the kitchen.

"Hi, honey," her mother said.

"Hello!" Cressida said. Then she turned to the unicorns and whispered, "My parents don't believe in unicorns, so they won't be able to see you."

All eight unicorn princesses filed through the door and into Cressida's living room. They walked slowly, mouths wide open as they stared at everything they saw.

"Look how small the couches and chairs are!" Firefly said.

"And look at this strange stuff on the floor," Moon said, pushing a hoof gently into the light blue carpet.

"How odd that there are no chandeliers," Breeze said, looking at the bare ceiling and then at the floor lamps.

"And there are no curtains," Prism said, staring at the blinds.

Cressida giggled.

"What is that terrible smell?" Bloom asked, wrinkling her nose.

"That's what my parents are making for dinner," Cressida explained. "It's spaghetti with tomato sauce and roasted carrots."

"Cressida, did you say something?" her father called out from the kitchen.

"I just said that dinner smells really good," Cressida said, winking at Bloom. Then, she whispered to the unicorns, "Come on! I'll show you my bedroom."

102

With the unicorn princesses right behind her, Cressida walked through the kitchen and down the hall that led to her bedroom.

"Grown-up humans are so much taller than human girls," Flash said.

"And how strange that there's a kitchen without any dragons in it," Firefly said.

Cressida opened her bedroom door, and all eight unicorns walked inside. She closed the door behind them. "Look at all these unicorn paintings and sculptures!" Prism said, admiring the watercolor unicorn pictures on the walls and all the unicorn sculptures Cressida had made of milk cartons, paper towel rolls, pipe cleaners, string, and straws.

103

"And look at this unicorn lamp!" Flash said.

"And this unicorn rug!" Breeze said.

"There's even a unicorn bedspread," Moon said.

"And a unicorn nightlight," Sunbeam said.

"And a unicorn clock," Prism said.

"I think there are more unicorns in here than in the Rainbow Realm," Firefly said.

Cressida giggled.

"It is so much fun to go on an adventure," Sunbeam said.

"I'm thrilled we could all go together," Feather said.

"I'm very glad," Cressida said. She put her magic key, which was still in her jeans pocket, back in her bedside table drawer. Then, she put the bottle of magic potion and her pictures of the Rainbow Realm on top of her bureau. "We can use these whenever you're ready to go home," Cressida said. "But I sure do hope you'll stay for at least a little while."

"Absolutely," Feather said. "This is already the best adventure I've ever been on. And I've been on a lot of adventures!"

Just then, the doorbell rang.

"Stay right here!" Cressida said, jumping up. "I'll be right back."

Cressida raced out her bedroom door, down the hall, and up to the front door. She opened it, and there stood Gillian with her mother and Eleanor with her father.

105

Both girls were carrying sleeping bags and backpacks.

"Hello!" Cressida said, hopping with excitement. "There's something I cannot wait to show you in my room!"

"Really?" Gillian said.

"Let's go!" Eleanor said.

Gillian, Eleanor, and Cressida raced down the hall. When they got to Cressida's closed door, Cressida said, "I need to just make sure of one thing. Do you believe in unicorns?"

Gillian smiled. "My mother always tells me they're not real. But I don't believe her."

"Unicorns are definitely real," Eleanor said.

"Great," Cressida said. "Now close your eyes."

Gillian and Eleanor shut their eyes. Cressida opened her bedroom door. "Now take three big steps forward."

Both girls walked into Cressida's bedroom.

Cressida closed the door. She winked at the unicorn princesses. And then she said, "Now you can look!"

Gillian and Eleanor opened their eyes.

"No way!" Gillian said. "Are those stuffed animals?"

"I promise they're real and alive!" Cressida said.

Eleanor's jaw dropped. And then she

began to giggle. "This is the most amazing thing I've ever seen."

"I feel like I'm in a dream," Gillian said.

"These are my friends Sunbeam, Flash, Bloom, Prism, Breeze, Moon, Firefly, and Feather. They're visiting from the Rainbow Realm," Cressida explained. "And these are my two best human friends, Gillian and Eleanor."

"Now we have three human friends!" Sunbeam said, grinning.

"It's wonderful to meet you," Flash said.

"They talk!" Eleanor shrieked, laughing and jumping up and down.

"This is incredible," Gillian said. She looked at the unicorns. She took a deep breath. "It's wonderful to meet you," she said.

"Thank you so much for coming to our sleepover," Eleanor said.

"Thank you for having us," Breeze said.

"This is absolutely amazing," Bloom added.

Just then, there was a knock on the door. "Don't worry," Cressida whispered to Gillian and Eleanor. "Only people who believe in unicorns can see them!"

Cressida opened the door. Her father stood with a plate of chocolate chip cookies. "I thought you girls might like these! Just don't eat too many before dinner."

"Thank you!" Cressida said.

"You're welcome," her father said, and he smiled and walked away.

Cressida closed the door and turned to her friends.

"Those look really good," Eleanor said.

"Did you make them yourself?" Gillian asked.

"I sure did," Cressida said. "Want to try them?"

"Sure!" Gillian and Eleanor said at once.

Then Gillian looked at the unicorns. "Do you want some, too?"

"Okay," Sunbeam said, sounding uncertain.

"It never hurts to try," Feather said.

"Hopefully we'll like them more than you like froyananas!" Bloom said.

Cressida held the plate out for Gillian, Eleanor, and each of the unicorns.

"These are great!" Gillian said, after she took a bite.

"They sure are," Eleanor said, nodding.

Cressida looked at the princess unicorns. They were all grimacing and frowning as they chewed and swallowed.

111

"I think we'll stick to froyananas and roinkleberries," Bloom said.

"But thank you for letting us try them," Feather added.

Cressida giggled. "No problem," she said. "Were they at least better than seaweed juice?"

Feather blushed. "I think they were worse!" she confessed.

Cressida, Gillian, Eleanor, Sunbeam, Flash, Bloom, Prism, Breeze, Moon, Firefly, and Feather all burst out laughing.

Cressida looked at her human friends and her unicorn friends. She smiled. And then she said, "Want to play a game?"

"Yes!" Gillian and Eleanor said at once.

"Definitely!" Sunbeam said.

"How about Telephone?" Eleanor suggested.

"Good idea," Gillian and Cressida said.

The eight unicorn princesses looked at each other with puzzled expressions and shrugged. "We'd really love to play," Feather said, "but we don't know how."

"We'd be happy to teach you," Cressida said. She quickly explained that one of them would start by whispering a sentence into the ear of the person—or unicorn!—next to her. That person or unicorn would repeat what she heard to whoever was sitting next to her. And they would keep doing that until the sentence had been whispered all the way around the circle.

"Let's try it!" Bloom said.

"I always love learning new games," Sunbeam said.

The other unicorns nodded.

"Why don't you start?" Gillian said, looking at Cressida.

Cressida blushed. "Okay," she said. She thought for a moment. And then she leaned

to her right and whispered, "I'm so happy my friends are here," into Eleanor's ear. Eleanor leaned over to Gillian, and whispered into her ear. Gillian whispered into Sunbeam's ear. Sunbeam giggled and whispered into Flash's ear. Flash leaned over and whispered to Bloom, who whispered to Prism, who whispered to Breeze, who whispered to Moon, who whispered to Firefly, who finally whispered to Feather.

"Now, Feather says what she heard from Firefly," Gillian said.

Feather blushed. I heard, "Froyanana cookies sure would taste better!"

Cressida laughed. "And I said, 'I'm so happy my friends are here.'"

The human girls and the unicorn

princesses all burst out laughing. Cressida felt her heart swell with joy as she looked around her. Her very best friends—both from the human world and the Rainbow Realm—were all right there in her bedroom, and she couldn't think of anything better in the whole world.

Emily Bliss lives just down the street from a forest. From her living room window, she can see a big oak tree with a magic keyhole. Like Cressida Jenkins, she knows that unicorns are real.

Sydney Hanson was raised in Minnesota alongside numerous pets and brothers. She has worked for several animation shops, including Nickelodeon and Disney Interactive. In her spare time she enjoys traveling and spending time outside with her adopted brother, a Labrador retriever named Cash. She lives in Los Angeles.

www.sydwiki.tumblr.com

Princess Ponies
BY CHLOE RYDER

Don't miss Pippa's journey to find the golden horseshoes and save Chevalia!

Princess Ponies — A Magical Friend
Princess Ponies — A Dream Come True
Princess Ponies — The Special Secret
Princess Ponies — A Unicorn Adventure!
Princess Ponies — An Amazing Rescue
Princess Ponies — Best Friends Forever!
Princess Ponies — A Special Surprise
Princess Ponies — A Singing Star

www.bloomsbury.com
Facebook: KidsBloomsbury
Twitter: BloomsburyKids